PRiNCESS of PETS

The Lonely Pony

Swinging round, Bea saw Sandy beside the picnic table, nibbling at the flower sweets on top of the trifle. She stared at the pony. "Sandy! How did you get here?"

Look out for more of Princess Bea's adventures!

The Naughty Kitten

The Lost Puppy

The Snowy Reindeer

PRINCESS of PETS

The Lonely Pony

Paula Harrison

Illustrated by
Olivia Chin Mueller

nosy
crow

For Brian and Stephanie, thanks for all the roast dinners and scrumptious desserts.

First published in the UK in 2020 by Nosy Crow Ltd
The Crow's Nest, 14 Baden Place,
Crosby Row, London SE1 1YW

Nosy Crow and associated logos are trademarks and/or registered
trademarks of Nosy Crow Ltd

1 3 5 7 9 10 8 6 4 2

A CIP catalogue record for this book is available from the British Library

Printed and bound in the UK by Clays Ltd, Elcograf S.p.A.

Papers used by Nosy Crow are made from wood grown in
sustainable forests.

ISBN: 978 1 78800 472 5

www.nosycrow.com

Chapter One
The Pony on the Shore

Bea skipped along Savara Beach, loving the warmth of the golden sand beneath her toes. In the distance a fishing boat was gliding across the sea. The water glittered as the wind whipped up little white-foamed waves. Seagulls circled over the cliffs, calling loudly. Bea began to run towards the ocean, the sea breeze lifting her dark curly hair.

"Wait for me!" Her brother, Alfie, chased after her.

"Princess Beatrice! Prince Alfred!" called Nancy. "I'll be sitting over here. Make sure you keep out of the waves. If your clothes get wet Mrs Stickler will be cross with all of us." The palace maid settled down on a picnic rug at the top of the beach. She folded her hands over her apron and gave a contented sigh. The palm trees that lined the seafront waved gently behind her.

Bea didn't see the point of coming to the seaside without getting wet. She jumped into a sandy rock pool and salt water splashed all over her shorts and T-shirt. It was a lovely hot day and she was sure her clothes would dry quickly. Mrs Stickler, the bossy royal housekeeper, would never find out.

Alfie and Bea lived at Ruby Palace with their father, King George, and their older sister, Natasha. The palace, with its beautiful golden towers, sat high on the top of the hill outside the village. It had an enormous garden with stables for the royal horses and an orchard full of lemon and plum trees.

Even though it was the summer holidays, King George was still busy with important royal matters, so Bea, Natasha and Alfie had lots of time to do what they liked. Natasha, who wanted to become the best pianist in the Kingdom of Neravia, had been playing the piano for most of the morning. Alfie had been making a mud concoction in a corner of the vegetable plot.

Bea had spent the morning climbing trees with Tiger, the beautiful stripy ginger kitten that roamed the palace garden. Tiger loved climbing but he was much better at going up than down. Sometimes he would get stuck at the top of a tree. Then he would meow pitifully, his furry face peering out between the branches, until Bea carried him down again.

After rescuing Tiger three times, Bea had begun teaching the little cat how to climb down by himself. It had been a fun morning but after lunch Mrs Stickler had, sent her indoors.

"I really cannot start preparing for the Royal Garden Party with you jumping about the place, Princess Beatrice," the housekeeper had said. "I have a million things to do before all the guests arrive tomorrow so please go inside and let me get on."

Bea went in reluctantly. The Royal Garden Party only happened once a year and it was always lots of fun. The king had invited everyone in the village to come and be part of the special occasion. There would be games and a wonderful spread of food, and prizes for those people who'd done something special to help others during the year.

Bea had wanted to help get everything ready, but Mrs Stickler wore such a grumpy look that she didn't like to ask. She'd persuaded Nancy to take her and Alfie to the beach instead, and they had hurried out of the royal gate before Mrs Stickler could protest.

Shading her eyes, Bea looked around the beach eagerly. Sometimes she would meet her best friend, Keira, down here. Keira's gorgeous puppy, Rosie, liked

running around on the sand and barking
at the waves. Bea loved all animals, but
she was especially fond of Rosie. She'd
found the little dog lost in the palace
garden a few months ago. Rosie had
needed lots of careful looking after and
Bea thought she was the sweetest puppy
in the world!

Bea really wanted a pet of her own
but every time she begged her dad for
a hamster or a dog, or even a tortoise,
he would shake his head. "Beatrice, the
palace is no place for a pet," he would
tell her, explaining that important
guests would be shocked if there were
animals running around all over the
place.

Without a pet of her own, Bea had
begun looking for any animals that
needed her help. She had started with

Fluff, the little mouse she'd found living in a tiny hole behind the piano in the dining room, and she'd also rescued a family of doves whose tree had blown down in a storm.

Rosie the puppy and Tiger the kitten were two of her latest rescues. Rosie had grown a lot bigger since Bea first found her, but she still bounded towards Bea wagging her tail every time they met. There was no sign of Keira or Rosie on the beach today. The place was quite empty apart from Nancy, who was dozing on the picnic rug, and two squabbling boys who were being marched away from the water by their mum.

Alfie found a stick and started poking about in a rock pool, moving the seaweed around. Bea followed the shoreline, looking for shells. She especially liked the round pink ones that were smooth inside. Last time she'd come to the beach she'd gone back home with a whole pocketful.

She walked past a cluster of tall rocks where she and Alfie sometimes liked to play pirates. She was peering at the sand so hard that she didn't spot the little grey-and-white pony until she was quite close. She stopped suddenly, her heart skipping. The little horse was standing all alone beside the water, the breeze lifting her soft grey mane.

Bea looked around, expecting to see the horse's owner, but there was no one else nearby. She took a few steps closer, but the pony twitched her ears in alarm and backed away. Bea tried again, walking very slowly and holding out her hand. She had learned to approach the horses in the royal stables this way so that they didn't get nervous. The pony snuffled at Bea's hand and shook her mane.

"Hello, you're lovely, aren't you?" Bea stroked the pony's velvety coat and noticed that the animal was quite dusty and her mane was full of tangles.

The pony gave a soft whinny and nudged her shoulder gently. Bea stared all around the beach but no one seemed to be looking for the little horse. She noticed the creature wasn't wearing a saddle or a bridle either.

"You must belong to someone." Bea rubbed the pony's soft neck. "I wonder how you came to be here all by yourself!"

"Princess Beatrice!" called Nancy, hurrying down the beach. "What are you doing with that pony? There's no time for

messing around. Mrs Stickler probably expected us back hours ago."

"She seems to be here all alone so I was wondering who she belongs to," Bea explained. "Have you seen anyone looking for a pony?"

"I don't think so." Nancy stared round distractedly. "We really must get going. Mrs Stickler will need me to set the table for dinner. Prince Alfie! We have to go now."

Alfie waved the stick covered in seaweed over his head like a flag. "But you promised us an ice cream!"

"Oh dear! I'd forgotten about that." Nancy brushed sand off her skirt. "Hurry up then! We'll buy an ice cream on the way."

Alfie dashed up the beach, trailing the seaweed stick behind him.

"I'll catch up with you," Bea told the royal maid. "I'm just going to make sure the pony gets back to her owner."

"Well, don't be long! Dinner will be at half past five," Nancy called back.

Bea gazed around the beach as Nancy and Alfie disappeared along the road to the ice cream shop. The two boys she'd spotted with their mother had gone and the only people left on the shoreline were an elderly couple walking along hand-in-hand. Bea walked up the beach, hoping to find more people she could ask about the pony.

To her surprise, the little horse trotted after her and nibbled at her hair.

"That tickles!" Bea said, laughing. "You're very friendly, aren't you?"

The pony whinnied and tossed her

head. Then she lay down and rolled back

and forth. When she leapt up again, she was covered in sand.

"That's what I'll call you – Sandy!" Bea smiled. "It suits you."

The pony swished her tail and blew

in Bea's ear. When Bea looked around the beach again, the elderly couple had left and the seafront was empty. The sun was turning a fiery orange as it sank towards the sparkling sea.

Bea stroked the pony's velvet coat, desperately trying to decide what to do. How had the pony come to be here all by itself? She couldn't leave the creature alone on the beach, but she really had to get back to Ruby Palace. Then a crazy idea popped into her head.

"You can't stay here on your own after dark," she told Sandy. "You'll have to come back to the palace with me. I can look after you until I find out where you came from." She held out her hand and the pony followed her up the beach.

Bea's heart skipped with excitement as she led Sandy along the path that took them back to Ruby Palace. There were lots of horses in the royal stables but they were enormous creatures and Bea had to stand on tiptoe just to stroke their manes. They were mainly kept for pulling the king's carriage, which was used on special occasions.

Sandy was just the right size for Bea. She had a soft, smooth coat and Bea loved the cheeky way the pony nibbled her hair. She couldn't wait to take Sandy back to Ruby Palace and look after her!

Chapter Two

The Hoof Prints in the Garden

Bea opened the palace gate and the pony trotted happily into the royal garden. As Bea closed the gate again, Sandy set off, cantering up the drive towards the front door as if she wanted to gallop right inside the palace.

"Sandy, wait!" Bea ran after the pony, catching her just as she reached the fountain.

Rows of tables were set out on the

grass, ready for the Royal Garden Party the next day. Chairs were lined up in rows and there were rolled-up sun umbrellas ready to offer some shade.

Bea coaxed the pony across the lawn towards the royal stables as quickly as she could. The sky was growing darker and she knew that if she wasn't on time for dinner she would get asked a lot of tricky questions. If she was really late, Mrs Stickler might even come looking for her. If the housekeeper saw Sandy, she would be sure to tell King George. Then her dad would want to know why she'd brought a strange pony to the palace.

She would sneak Sandy into the stables for the night and then fetch her early the next morning before the grooms were up. Then they'd return to the beach to look for the pony's owner.

"Here we are, Sandy!" Bea led the
pony across the stable yard. "I'll find
you a stall with some hay and some
water." She pushed at the stable door but
it was locked and the yard was empty.

Bea frowned. She needed to find a
comfortable place for Sandy to stay and
time was running out. "I know! You can
stay in the orchard tonight."

Sandy tossed her head and whinnied
softly as she followed Bea to the orchard
gate. Mrs Cherry, the royal gardener,
had built a fence to keep the orchard,
with all its lemon and plum trees,
separate from the rest of the garden.
Bea led Sandy inside and closed the gate
firmly. Then she found a bucket and
filled it with water. The pony would be
safe here with plenty of grass to eat.

Bea hugged the pony gently. "I wish

I didn't have to go! But I'll be back first thing in the morning. I promise."

Sandy nibbled Bea's hair before leaning down to graze the grass.

"Princess Beatrice!" Mrs Stickler's voice rang out across the garden.

Bea jumped. "Coming, Mrs Stickler." With one last glance at Sandy, she ran out of the orchard.

The housekeeper was standing at the front door. "Princess Beatrice, dinner is served and we've all been waiting for you. What on earth have you been doing? You're covered in sand."

"Sorry!" Bea brushed the sand off her T-shirt. It must have got there when she'd hugged the pony.

"Well there's no time to get changed," grumbled Mrs Stickler. "Take your sandals off – as quick as you can."

Bea meekly followed the housekeeper into the dining room. At least she'd found a safe place for Sandy to sleep, and tomorrow she would take the little pony something special for breakfast.

Bea planned to get up early and visit
Sandy before anyone else was awake,
but when she opened her eyes sunlight
was already streaming through the
curtains. An engine rumbled and Bea
peeked outside to see a delivery van
pulling up to the back door. Darou, the
palace chef, came running out of the
kitchen, waving his arms frantically.

Bea pulled on her jeans and a T-shirt
and hurried downstairs. The kitchen
was buzzing as the maids rushed to
and fro carrying boxes of strawberries,
cherries and plums, and enormous tubs
of different flavoured ice creams. Bea
waited till no one was looking before
sneaking inside and taking a handful of
carrots. Then she darted out of the back

door into the garden, her heart racing.

She'd forgotten that the garden party was today. What if someone had already been into the orchard and found Sandy?

Mrs Stickler was outside, wiping the party tables with a cloth. "Good morning, Princess Beatrice. What on earth are you doing with those carrots?"

Bea's mind whirled. "Um… Well I'm hungry and I know that carrots are really good for you…" The housekeeper frowned suspiciously so Bea took a big bite out of one of the carrots.

"You need to eat a proper breakfast." Mrs Stickler scrubbed at a dirty mark on the table. "Skipping round the garden eating carrots is more suited to rabbits than princesses!"

Mrs Cherry came past with her

wheelbarrow. "Morning, Princess Bea! Which flowers would you like for the tables, Mary? I think roses would look nice."

The two women began talking about flowers. Bea turned to go but stopped when she heard Mrs Cherry say, "And isn't it strange about the hoof prints in the vegetable garden? Something's eaten half of the cucumbers but the grooms say all the horses were locked in their stalls last night."

Bea's heart sank. Surely the cucumber-stealer couldn't be Sandy! The little pony had been shut safely in the orchard.

She slipped away and ran to the orchard gate. "Sandy?" she whispered. "I've brought you some carrots."

But there was no sign of Sandy and

when Bea searched among the trees she found part of the fence was newly broken. Bea rubbed her forehead worriedly.

Sandy must have escaped, and the palace garden was so huge that the pony could be anywhere. She had to find the creature before she did any more damage.

Remembering what Mrs Cherry had said about mysterious hoof prints, Bea raced towards the vegetable plot. She was halfway across the garden when there was a loud screech. A moment later, Natasha ran outside.

"Mrs Stickler, come quickly!" she cried.

"What's wrong, Princess Natasha? Are you hurt?" The housekeeper rushed up the steps.

"There's a cow or something outside the parlour window," Natasha said breathlessly. "It was pressing its nose right up against the glass. I only caught a glimpse of it before it disappeared."

"A cow!" exclaimed Mrs Stickler. "I don't believe it. There can't be a cow in the garden. How would it get over the palace walls?"

"There was!" cried Natasha. "It had big eyes and a long nose with huge nostrils."

Bea raced round the side of the palace and found Sandy nibbling at the roses under the parlour window. The pony tossed her head as Bea came rushing around the corner.

Bea quickly held out a carrot. She had to get the pony out of sight. "It's all right, Sandy. Look, I brought some breakfast for you."

The pony trotted over and munched the carrot eagerly. Bea heard Natasha and Mrs Stickler approaching, so she tried to pull Sandy into the royal maze. The little pony shook her mane and refused to move.

"Come on, Sandy!" Bea's heart pounded as she offered another carrot. "You DO like these better than the flowers, don't you?"

Sandy pricked up her ears and at last she followed Bea into the maze, with its tall hedge walls.

"It can't have been a cow, Natasha. I think there's a horse on the loose. It's already left hoof prints all around the place," Mrs Stickler said crossly. "I shall speak to the grooms at once. On an important day like this they really need to keep their animals under control."

Natasha spotted Bea at the maze entrance. "What are you doing, Bea?"

Bea stuck the carrots in her pocket. "Nothing! Just going inside for breakfast."

"Yes, get some breakfast – both of you." Mrs Stickler shooed them up the palace steps. "When you've finished eating I'd like your help, please. There's ever so much to do."

"Yes, Mrs Stickler." Natasha tucked her hair behind her ears. "Of course we'll help."

Bea sighed as she followed her sister inside. If Mrs Stickler had her way, she would spend the day wiping tables and tidying the garden. All she really wanted to do was take Sandy to the beach to find her owner again.

Chapter Three
Sandy's Garden Adventure

Bea bolted down her breakfast and hurried out of the royal dining room. She hoped Sandy was still safely hidden in the maze. King George stopped her in the hall. "Morning, Beatrice! Are you excited about the party?"

"Yes, I can't wait!" said Bea, truthfully.

"Good! This is an important occasion for everyone," said her father. "It's the one day each year where we thank the people of Savara for all the wonderful things they do. Would you like to help me give out the prizes later?"

"Yes, please!" Bea glanced at the door. She really had to return to Sandy before the pony trotted away, leaving more hoof prints everywhere.

The king smiled. "Well, off you go and give Mrs Stickler a hand. I'm sure she needs the help."

Bea hurried outside and headed straight for the maze. She'd almost reached it when Natasha called after her.

"Help me with these, Bea! Mrs Stickler wants more chairs and tables on this side of the garden." Natasha picked up a pile of chairs. "There are lots of people coming from Savara. It's quite exciting, isn't it?"

"I guess so!" Bea helped her sister move a table. She usually loved the Royal Garden Party. The food was always amazing. There would be sandwiches and sausage rolls, a fruit salad and some kind of special dessert.

Last year, Chef Darou had cooked five different kinds of cheesecake and decorated them all with fresh fruit. Bea had loved the mango one so much she'd had seconds, but this time she hadn't thought about the garden party at all. She could only think about Sandy.

Natasha handed Bea a white lace table cloth. "What's wrong, Bea? You're acting really strange today."

Bea hesitated. Natasha often thought being the eldest meant she was in charge. If she found out about Sandy, she was bound to go on and on about why there should be no pets in the palace.

Natasha looked at her sister more closely. "Bea? You haven't brought another animal inside, have you?"

"Not inside exactly…" Bea unfolded the table cloth and gave it a shake.

Just then, Sandy poked her nose out of the maze entrance and gave a loud whinny.

Natasha gaped. "Bea, you haven't—"

"Girls!" Mrs Stickler came rushing over with a basket full of roses and lilies. "Could you make up flower displays for the tables? And there's some bunting to be hung from the trees."

Bea panicked and held the table cloth up high, blocking Sandy from view. "Sorry! I'm busy with this right now…"

"Of course we'll do the flowers!" said Natasha in a rush. "Just leave it to us."

Mrs Stickler beamed. "Thank you, that's—" Sandy snorted loudly and the housekeeper broke off to glare at Bea. "What a horrible sneeze, Princess Beatrice. Perhaps you'd better go indoors and get a tissue."

"Yes, Mrs Stickler." Bea tried not to giggle as Sandy snuffled behind the table cloth.

Luckily the housekeeper hurried away to speak to Nancy, who had appeared with a large stack of picnic plates.

"Bea, where did that pony come from?" hissed Natasha. "It's much too small to be one from the stables."

"Her name's Sandy and she was all alone on the beach yesterday," Bea explained. "I had to bring her back here before it got dark. I'm taking her back to the beach to look for her owner."

Natasha sighed. "This is even worse than when you brought home the kitten!"

Bea eyed her sister closely. At least Natasha wasn't rushing off to tell Mrs Stickler. "I'll take her away soon, I promise. I was just about to go but Mrs Stickler made me do all this. You won't tell anyone, will you?"

"If you're really taking her straight back to the beach then I don't mind." Natasha gave Bea a stern look. "But that horse has got to be gone before the garden party starts. You know how important today is to everyone. Father's been preparing his speech all morning and Mrs Stickler has been planning everything for weeks."

Bea nodded eagerly. "Sandy will be

gone soon – I promise!"

"All right! Could you help me with the flowers and the bunting before you go?" Natasha took one end of the table cloth and together they spread it over the table.

Natasha cut the roses and lilies carefully and Bea put them into vases. Then they tied the bunting to the lower branches of the trees. The green and purple flags fluttered gently in the wind.

Bea suddenly spotted the pony nibbling at some of the roses. "Sandy, no!" She rushed to save them but the pony had chewed up every last petal. "Oops! I'd better ask Mrs Cherry for some more flowers."

"I'll go," sighed Natasha. "You should take that animal back to the beach. Her owner could be there looking for her. For goodness sake, take her away now before she eats everything!"

Bea turned back to find Sandy nibbling at the bunting. "Are you hungry, Sandy? Look what I've got!" She pulled a carrot out of her pocket and the pony trotted after her slowly. But as soon as Sandy had finished the carrot she stopped to graze the grass again.

Bea bit her lip. "It's going to take ages to get to the beach if I have to lure you there with carrots. We'd get there so much faster if I could ride you. Would you like that?" Her heart skipped nervously. She had been riding a few times on the huge royal horses but there had always been a groom beside her, ready to take the reins.

Sandy tossed her head and whickered gently. Bea drew the pony down the slope to the stables and hid her in an empty stall. Then she fetched some equipment from the tack room. She had never tacked up a horse by herself before, but she'd watched the grooms do it and she was sure she knew what to do.

Looping the headcollar over Sandy's nose, she fastened it carefully. Then she placed the saddle on to the pony's back and strapped everything into place. Sandy's ears pricked up and she swished her tail eagerly.

Last of all, Bea found a brush and tried to comb the tangles out of Sandy's beautiful mane. She longed to brush the pony's coat too but there wasn't time. Putting on a riding hat, she tightened the strap under her chin. Sandy shook her mane and whickered. Bea smiled. She'd never seen the pony so excited. Leading her out of the stables, Bea climbed into the saddle and took the reins.

Her stomach did a somersault and she took a deep breath. "All right, Sandy. Let's go!" She tapped the pony's side gently with her heels.

Sandy leapt forward with a long whinny. Bea's heart skipped as they trotted across the garden, keeping behind the trees. Riding Sandy was so much easier than riding any of the royal horses the grooms had let her try.

Natasha was waiting by the palace gate. "Go quickly!" she told Bea. "Mrs Stickler's gone inside to look for table napkins but she'll be back in a minute and there are maids everywhere."

"Thanks, Natasha." Bea looked at her sister in surprise.

"Don't be late back." Natasha pulled the gate open. "The garden party starts at two o'clock and I can't cover for you forever."

"I'll try not to take too long," Bea called back as Sandy dashed through the gate. She held the reins tight. The wind rushed past her and she felt like she was flying as Sandy galloped down the hill to Savara.

Chapter Four

Danger on the Sand

Bea rode all the way into Savara on Sandy's back. She pulled on the reins as they reached the bottom of the hill and the pony whinnied and slowed down into a walk. Bea smiled at everyone as she passed by. Mr Patel from the bakery waved at her. "See you at the garden party, Princess Beatrice!" he called.

"Yes, see you soon!" Bea smiled, careful not to let go of the reins in case she wobbled.

Bea guided the pony towards the seafront where palm trees fluttered in the breeze. Excitement fizzed inside her. This felt so smooth and easy, not bumpy like riding the enormous horses from the royal stables. She gently steered Sandy on to the warm golden sand. The sea sparkled brightly and the wind was whipping up little silver-tipped waves.

Bea jumped down and looped the reins around her hand. Sandy snorted and shook her pale mane. The little pony seemed so much happier now than she had been the day before. Her eyes were bright and her tail swished joyfully.

"Does your owner ride you all the time?" Bea asked Sandy softly. "You must really miss them." She looked around the beach, wondering if Sandy's owner was already here.

There was a family sitting on a picnic rug eating their lunch, and a boy and his grandma building a ring of sandcastles. None of the people paid any attention to Bea and Sandy. Bea suddenly wondered what Sandy's owner was like. Surely a good owner would have looked after the pony better and kept her safe.

Sandy whickered gently and nudged Bea's shoulder with her nose.

"Are you hungry?" Bea offered Sandy the last carrot out of her pocket but the pony didn't take it. She whinnied and bumped Bea's shoulder a second time.

"Do you want to go riding again?" asked Bea, smiling.

Sandy's ears pricked up, so Bea climbed back into the saddle and tapped her heels against the pony's sides. Sandy

swished her tail and cantered into
the shallows, sending up fountains of
sparkling spray with her hooves.

Bea laughed and tugged on the reins
as they drew closer to the cliff. Sandy
wheeled round and galloped back along
the sand. The wind whirled around them
and Bea felt like she was racing the
fluffy clouds scudding across the sky.

Sandy and Bea cantered up and
down the shore for a long time. At last
Bea looked at her watch. It was already
quarter past one and she still wasn't any
closer to finding Sandy's owner. Maybe
she should walk into the village and ask
if anyone had been searching for a lost
pony?

"Stay here, Sandy." She tied the
pony's reins to a post at the top of the
beach. "I'll be back really soon." She
stroked Sandy's nose but the pony stood
looking straight ahead.

Bea hurried along the street. She

didn't want to leave Sandy for too long. The pony had changed as soon as Bea had tied her reins to the post. Her ears had drooped and her tail had stopped moving. Maybe she hated being tethered.

Bea went into the bakery looking for Mr Patel. The baker was busy and as Bea stood waiting, there was a tap on her shoulder.

"Hello, Bea!" Keira smiled. "I didn't think I'd see you till the party."

"Hi Keira." Bea grinned. "Is Rosie with you?"

"No, my dad took her for a walk today. I'm just buying some things for the café and then I'm going back to get ready for the garden party." Keira held up a shopping bag with some oranges and tomatoes. Keira's family, the

Makalis, ran the Sleepy Gull Café on the clifftop, and Keira helped out there all the time.

"You've got to come and see my pony!" Bea said excitedly. "She's called Sandy and she's really cute."

"Did your dad let you have your own horse?" Keira's eyes widened.

"No, I found her all alone on the beach yesterday and I'm still looking for her owner." Bea grabbed Keira's arm and pulled her to the door. "She's such a sweet pony. Come and see!"

The girls hurried back to the beach. Bea was about to point Sandy out when she noticed the pony's head was raised and her ears were pinned back. Suddenly the little horse began pawing at the ground.

"Something's wrong!" Bea started running.

Sandy tossed her head fiercely and whinnied. A thin green shape twisted and coiled on the sand.

"There's a snake, Bea," called Keira. "Right there by her hooves."

The snake raised its pointed head into the air and its tongue flickered. Its body rippled as it slid closer to the pony's hooves.

"She must be scared of them," panted Bea. "Quick, before she panics!"

The pony rolled her eyes and pawed the ground again.

Bea recognised the snake's brown-and-green markings. She'd seen this kind of snake before on the cliff path and she knew it wasn't venomous. "Sandy, it's just a grass snake. It can't hurt you!"

The pony backed away, snorting, but she was tied fast to the post. The reins drew tight, straining against the wood. Sandy tossed her head again and the knot in the reins began to loosen. Bea rushed forward but the knot unravelled and, suddenly free, the pony galloped away across the beach.

"Sandy, wait!" called Bea. "Everything's going to be all right."

But Sandy only galloped faster.

Reaching the other side of the beach, she cantered up the narrow track that led through the bushes away from Savara. Soon the little pony was lost among the trees.

Bea stopped to catch her breath. "I didn't see a snake here when I left her. I never should have tied her to that post."

"It's not your fault." Keira put an arm around her friend. "You couldn't leave her loose either. Maybe she'll come back in a minute."

But the little pony didn't reappear. Bea's heart sank. Sandy was all alone again and she might keep on galloping for miles. What if it was impossible to find her?

Chapter Five
Silver Gate Farm

Keira and Bea scrambled up the narrow track where Sandy had disappeared. A rabbit scuttled into its burrow as they pushed past the thick prickly bushes. They crossed a tangled piece of scrubland scattered with wildflowers and followed a zig-zagging path up the slope. The beach grew smaller behind them.

They stopped at the top to catch their

breath. The track they'd followed joined the narrow road that led to Ruby Palace. Bea glanced right and left, wondering which way Sandy might have gone. To her right the gates of Ruby Palace were open and gleaming in the afternoon sunshine. The guests for the Royal Garden Party hadn't started arriving yet.

"Hey, these look like hoof prints." Keira pointed to a line of round marks on the dusty roadside.

Bea's heart leapt. "Then Sandy definitely came down here! But which way was she going?"

"This way I think." Keira pointed left to where the road led away from the palace.

Bea peered closely at the hoof marks. "She must have been so scared by that snake that she just kept galloping.

"I hope she hasn't got too far." Keira peered down the lane.

Bea looked back towards the palace gate. Guests would start arriving for the garden party very soon and she was meant to be there, dressed in her best clothes and ready to welcome everyone. She rubbed her forehead worriedly. She just had to search for Sandy first. The little pony could be in danger.

Keira and Bea hurried along the lane, following the hoof marks. The road grew narrower until it was just a dirt track with two deep grooves worn by the wheels of passing vehicles.

"Maybe it isn't an accident that Sandy came this way," Bea said suddenly. "What if this is where she lives?"

"It would be lovely if she's found her way home," said Keira.

"I guess so." Bea ducked under some low-hanging branches at the side of the lane. If Sandy had found her way home that *was* good ... but what if she never saw the little pony again?

Round the next corner the lane ended in a large gate hung with the sign *Silver Gate Farm*. An old farmhouse stood at the far side of a dusty yard. Behind the building there were several fields of brown and white cows but the nearest field had just one small cow grazing on the grass.

Bea climbed on to the gate and shaded her eyes. The cow standing all alone wasn't a cow at all. It was Sandy!

Keira spotted the pony at the exact same moment. "There she is! You were right, Bea. She must have known where she was going."

Bea took off her riding hat, Keira dropped her shopping bag on the grass and they both scrambled over the gate.

"Sandy, are you all right?" Bea ran across the paddock.

Sandy flattened her ears and backed away. Then she tossed her head and whinnied as the girls drew closer. Bea threw her arms around the pony's neck. "I'm sorry the snake scared you!"

The pony stayed quite still and when Bea released her, she backed away a little more.

"You've lost your saddle too," said Bea. "You must have galloped so fast it fell off! Maybe I didn't strap it on properly."

"She must have jumped over the fence to get back in." Keira stroked the pony gently. "That's quite a big jump for such a small pony!"

"We'd better tell the people that live here that she's come home. They must have missed her." Bea gazed around the empty farmyard. She couldn't shake off

the feeling that something wasn't right.
Why hadn't the farmer come out to meet
them?

The girls had just begun to climb over
the fence into the farmyard when a large
black dog rushed out of a barn, barking
wildly.

Bea stopped with one leg swung over
the fence. "Hello!" she called towards the
farmhouse. "Can you call off your dog?
We've come to talk to you."

"It's about your pony," added Keira.

But no one appeared and the dog
began growling and jumping up at the
fence.

"Maybe no one's home," said Keira.
"But we can come back and talk to
Sandy's owner later. At least she's safe
for now."

Bea frowned. "What if this is the

wrong place? I don't think I can leave Sandy here unless I know for sure that it's her real home."

"But she jumped right over the fence into this field!" said Keira. "I thought you wanted to find her owner."

"I do!" Bea flushed. "But how do we know she belongs here without speaking to anyone? I think I should take her back to the palace."

Keira patted the pony's neck. "Don't you think you're just trying to keep the pony for yourself?"

"I'm not!" Bea shook back her curly dark hair. "I'm trying to do the best thing for Sandy."

Keira put her hand on Bea's arm. "Don't be cross, Bea! It's just that she seems so happy here. Why don't we come back and check on her after the garden party?"

Bea sighed. "I guess you're right."
She checked her watch. "Uh oh! I said
I'd be back by two o'clock for the party
and it's half past two already." She gave
the pony another hug. "Bye, Sandy! I
promise I'll check on you later."

Sandy gave a snort and went back
to grazing the grass. Keira and Bea
climbed over the fence and ran back
down the lane. When they reached the
palace gates, people were pouring into
the royal garden wearing their best
clothes and sun hats. Even more people
were streaming up the hill from Savara
and many of them were carrying salads
and baskets of cupcakes to add to the
picnic food. There was a happy buzz of
chatter.

"Look, it's Princess Beatrice returning

for the party," said Mr Patel. "Make way, everyone! Have you been off on an adventure, Princess Beatrice?"

Bea blushed as she and Keira walked inside. "We were helping a lost pony," she told him. She suddenly wondered whether Mr Patel knew who owned Silver Gate Farm. "Do you know who lives at the farm just down the lane – the one with all the cows?"

The baker looked puzzled. "I'm not sure I know which one you mean, Princess Beatrice. Which direction was it?"

Bea was just about to explain when Alfie dashed up to them. "I've been looking for you for ages!" he panted. "Mrs Stickler's gone wild because she can't find you. You'd better hurry up."

Bea glanced down at her grubby jeans. The housekeeper would be even crosser once she saw the state of her clothes and there wasn't time to sneak inside to change. Bea tried to drag her fingers through her tangled hair. How could she explain being covered in dust at the most important royal occasion of the whole year?

Chapter Six

The Trouble with Trifle

Bea brushed hastily at her T-shirt as she made her way across the garden. Her fingers were so dusty that she didn't know if she was making things worse. King George was standing by the palace steps, smiling and shaking the guests' hands. Bea crossed her fingers that he didn't look too closely at her clothes.

"Beatrice, there you are!" King George boomed. "Hello Keira! Are your parents here too?"

"They're just finishing the lunch orders at the café. They'll be here really soon," said Keira, bobbing a curtsy.

"That's excellent!" The king smiled broadly. "Why don't you girls get some food? The ham rolls are very tasty."

Bea's stomach rumbled, reminding her that she hadn't eaten any lunch yet. By the time she and Keira had made their way through the crowd to the picnic table, Mrs Stickler had disappeared into the palace kitchen with a stack of empty plates.

Bea picked up a roll and some cucumber and carrot sticks. The carrots reminded her of Sandy again and she felt a twist of sadness. Sandy was such an adorable pony. She hoped whoever lived at Silver Gate Farm would look after her

properly. As soon as the garden party
was over, she'd go back and check on her.

"Are you all right, Bea?" said Keira,
picking up a pizza slice. "Ooh, look at
those flowers! I think something's chewed
them."

Bea looked up quickly. The roses in
each vase had been chewed almost down
to the stalks. Natasha was supposed to
have thrown out the flowers that Sandy
had eaten and replaced them with new
ones. "That's weird! I wonder…" She
broke off as Mrs Stickler came out of the
kitchen carrying a vast dessert dish filled
with the largest and most amazing trifle
that Bea had ever seen.

It was a huge wobbling concoction of
plum jelly and chocolate sponge, topped
with extravagant swirls of cream. Multi-
coloured flower sweets were scattered

over the top like a bouquet. There was a gasp from the crowd followed by murmurs of admiration.

Natasha followed Mrs Stickler with a large stack of bowls. "I decorated the top of the trifle," she told everyone proudly.

Bea edged closer to her sister, whispering, "Natasha, didn't you change the flowers after I left?"

Natasha wasn't really listening. "Mind out, Bea! I don't want to drop these."

Mrs Stickler placed the dessert dish carefully on the table. Then she spotted Bea and frowned. "Why haven't you brushed your hair, Princess Beatrice? And what happened to the nice dress you were going to wear?"

Bea shuffled her feet. "I meant to go and get changed but I got really busy and—" She broke off, catching sight of something over the housekeeper's shoulder.

Two ladies stood talking beside the maze entrance. One was wearing a yellow hat decorated with large pink daisies. Bea watched as some of the flowers were whisked into the air and then disappeared behind the hedge.

"Bea!" Natasha nudged her. "Mrs

Stickler's talking to you."

"Oh, sorry!" Bea peered at the lady
with the daisy hat. For a second, she
thought she'd seen pony ears sticking
up behind the hedge, but that was
impossible! They'd left Sandy safe and
sound at the farm. There was no way the
pony could have trotted into the royal
garden without lots of people noticing.

King George tapped his glass.
"Gather round, everyone! I'd just like to
say a few words before we all try out this
delicious trifle."

Everyone gathered around the king.

"First of all, I'd like to thank you all
for coming," the king said. "Secondly,
I must thank Mrs Stickler for all her
hard work – for the food and the flower
displays." Bea looked doubtfully at the
vases of chewed flowers. "Thirdly, I'd like

to thank Princess Natasha and Princess
Beatrice who helped out and…"

Bea became distracted by a loud
slurping noise behind her. Swinging
round, she saw Sandy beside the picnic
table, nibbling at the flower sweets on
top of the trifle. She stared at the pony.
"Sandy! How did you get here?"

Mrs Stickler gave a loud shriek and
tried to shoo the pony away, but Sandy
was enjoying the plum jelly and cream
too much to move. "Get away, you
horrible animal! That's it – I'm fetching
the grooms." She marched off towards
the stables.

"What on earth is that pony doing in
my garden?" exclaimed King George.
"It's certainly not one of my horses."

"Bea!" Natasha hissed under her
breath. "I thought you took the pony
away. I told you it had to be gone before
the party."

"I did take it away!" Bea hissed back.

"What's that?" The king looked at his
daughters, a frown growing on his face.
"Girls, do you know something about all
this?"

"This is Sandy and I found her all

alone on the beach yesterday," explained Bea. "When I couldn't find her owner I brought her back here for the night, but I think she lives at a farm down the road. I left her there just now – I really don't know how she got back here!"

Sandy whinnied and began chewing some roses. Her nose was covered with cream and jelly. The two ladies standing by the maze shook their heads disapprovingly. A little boy in a red sun hat pointed at the pony and giggled.

"Beatrice, you really must learn to think!" said King George sternly. "Ponies have no place at a royal garden party."

Sandy tossed her head, nervous at the raised voices. She trotted into the crowd, making the guests scatter left and right. Then she gave a huge snort, covering

Natasha's dress with trifle. Natasha
gave a shriek. Grabbing a napkin, she
dabbed at the spilled cream and jelly.

Bea stared in horror at the streaks of

purple and white across her sister's dress. "Sandy! Come here." She took hold of the pony and tried to lead her away. "I'm really sorry everyone!"

Mrs Stickler returned with two grooms and ordered them to take Sandy to the stables. "I've called Stray Animal Services and they'll be here in half an hour," she informed the king. "They're bringing a horse trailer to take the animal away."

King George nodded approvingly. The grooms took hold of Sandy's broken reins and led her towards the stables.

Bea swallowed. Sandy would be taken away in half an hour! After that she'd probably never see the little pony again.

"And Princess Beatrice," added Mrs Stickler, "We're going to need a lot more napkins to clear up this mess. Please fetch them for me."

"Yes, Mrs Stickler." Bea turned to her father. "But Dad! Can't we keep Sandy for a little while longer? She's a great pony and she loves being ridden."

"That's enough, Beatrice!" King George's face darkened like a thunder cloud. "I'm very disappointed that you didn't care about our garden party. There will be no more unexpected animals brought into Ruby Palace. Now do as Mrs Stickler asks at once."

Bea's cheeks turned scarlet as she hurried away. She had never seen her dad look so cross before. If he didn't forgive her for bringing Sandy to Ruby Palace, this could be the end of her helping animals forever.

Chapter Seven

A Pony Surprise

Bea fetched the napkins from inside and mopped up the spilled trifle on the picnic table. When she tried to follow the grooms taking Sandy to the stables, Mrs Stickler stopped her. "No, Princess Beatrice. Let the grooms deal with this now, please."

The housekeeper rushed off to help Natasha find another dress to wear. Tears pricked Bea's eyes.

"Bea!" Keira grabbed her arm. "I've just realised I left my whole bag of shopping by the farm gate. I put it down before we climbed over the fence to see Sandy and accidentally left it there. Will you help me fetch it?"

Bea nodded, grateful to her friend for giving her a reason to leave the party and escape all the disapproving glances. Maybe by the time she got back everyone would have calmed down. As she trailed out of the palace gate after Keira, her dad's words echoed in her ears: *Beatrice, you really must learn to think!*

Her cheeks reddened again as she thought about Sandy eating the magnificent trifle. She'd only wanted to look after the pony. How had everything gone so wrong?

"I STILL don't understand how Sandy

got into your garden," said Keira for the third time. "We left her right there in the field."

"I don't understand either," sighed Bea. "But now my dad thinks I don't care about the garden party and that's not true!"

They turned the corner and the lane became a dirt track leading to the farm. Bea stopped by the farm gate to pick up Keira's shopping bag. Her riding hat was lying there too.

"Bea – look!" Keira grabbed her friend's arm.

Bea turned around and her stomach did a somersault.

Sandy was standing right where they'd left her. She raised her head to look at the girls, flicking her left ear.

"How did she get there?" cried Bea.

"It's like magic! One minute she's at the palace and the next minute she's here again."

Keira shook her head. "This is really strange. Sandy should be in the stables with those grooms."

Bea hooked the shopping bag over her arm and climbed the fence into Sandy's field. The pony bent her head to graze the grass. Her soft dapple-grey coat gleamed in the summer sunshine.

Suddenly things began to fit together in Bea's head like the pieces of a jigsaw. "Do you remember that Sandy lost her saddle?" she began slowly, "And we thought it had fallen off when she ran away from the grass snake?"

"I remember," said Keira. "Will your dad be cross that it's lost?"

Bea shook her head. "It's not that! I think Sandy was wearing the saddle when we saw her at the palace just now."

Keira looked puzzled. "But that makes no sense! Where has it gone?"

"I think Sandy's still wearing it — back at the palace." Bea pushed back her tangled curls. "I think there are two ponies that look the same. They're probably sisters!"

"So ... you're saying that Sandy's the one at the palace wearing the saddle and this pony is her sister?" Keira frowned.

"I think so! When Sandy left the beach she must have galloped straight into the palace garden before any of the

guests arrived. Then we followed the
hoof prints in the wrong direction and
ended up here ... and when we saw this
pony we thought it was Sandy!"

Keira nodded slowly. "That would
explain how the pony seemed to be in
two places at once! But what are we
going to do now? Mrs Stickler's already
rung Stray Animal Services and they'll
take Sandy away."

"I know – we haven't got long."
Bea chewed her lip. "I'm going to try
knocking on the farmhouse door."

Keira nodded "Be careful of the dog!"
The little pony trotted over and nuzzled
her shoulder. Keira smiled and rubbed
the animal's nose. "I'll stay here and
keep an eye on the pony."

Bea scrambled over the fence into the
yard, ran to the farmhouse door and

knocked firmly. She saw Keira waving
at her and quickly waved back. The door
opened and an old man with wispy grey
hair peered out.

"Sorry to disturb you!" said Bea
nervously. "I'm Bea and that's my friend,
Keira. I live at Ruby Palace."

"You're one of the princesses, aren't
you?" The man scratched his head and
grinned. "Well, it isn't every day that I get
a royal visit!"

"I was wondering whether you'd lost a
pony," continued Bea. "I found one on the
beach and—"

"What's that? Have you seen my pony,
Bella?" The man opened the door wider.
"I've been looking for her everywhere.
Bunty hasn't been the same without her. I
think she's pining!"

"Is Bunty the name of the other pony?"

Bea jerked back
suddenly as a
dog came rushing
out of the door,
barking loudly.

"Get down,
Casper!" The
man took hold of
the dog's collar. "Don't worry, he wouldn't
hurt a fly. I'm Mr Morley."

Bea quickly told Mr Morley how she'd
found Sandy on the beach and how she
had looked after her until the little horse
had taken fright at the snake and ran
away. "So, when we found your farm we
got mixed up and thought your other
pony was Sandy," she added. "They look
so similar."

"They're twins," Mr Morley told her. "I
bought them for my granddaughters to

ride, but when my son got a new job their family had to move away from Savara. Since then the ponies have been restless — especially Bella. She loves to be ridden." He gave a deep sigh. "I'd love to spend more time with them but I have all my cows to take care of. Anyway, yesterday I left the gate ajar by mistake and Bella disappeared."

Bea nodded. "That explains how she got loose." She took a deep breath. "Do you think my friend and I could take your other pony, Bunty, to the palace? I need to show her to my dad so that I can explain everything. The trouble is that Sandy, I mean Bella, could be taken away by Stray Animal Services any minute now!"

"You'd better hurry then," said Mr Morley. "I'll drive along in my van and meet you at the palace."

While Mr Morley looked for his van keys, Bea raced back to Keira. "I was right – there are two ponies!" she panted. "This one's called Bunty and we can take her back to the palace to explain."

"It might be too late." Keira looked at her watch. "That's why I was waving at you. They were taking the other pony away in half an hour and that time's nearly gone!"

Bea stroked Bunty's nose. Her brain spun like a fairground ride. "Then I'll just have to ride back! It'll be quicker." She handed Keira the shopping bag and grabbed the riding hat that she'd left on the ground. Then she scrambled on to the pony's back.

She'd never ridden without a saddle before and the pony's coat felt smooth

and slippery. She remembered how easy
it had been riding Sandy that morning.
She knew she could do this! She threaded
her fingers through Bunty's mane.

Bunty looked round in surprise and
whinnied happily. Keira opened the
gate leading to the lane. Bea tapped the
pony's sides gently and Bunty jumped
forwards, her tail swishing.

"I'll meet you there!" Bea called
to Keira. Then she leaned forward to
whisper into the pony's ear. "Come on,
Bunty! We're going to save your sister."

The pony whickered and broke into
a canter, her hooves thudding on the
ground. Bea's dark curls bounced on her
shoulders as they sped towards Ruby
Palace.

Chapter Eight

Bella and Bunty

Bea's heart sank when she saw a horse trailer parked outside the palace gates. Someone from Stray Animal Services must already have arrived. Soon they would take Sandy away.

Bunty stopped outside the gates and tossed her head nervously. There was a buzz of voices from inside the royal garden.

"It's all right, Bunty!" Bea spoke

soothingly and patted the pony's neck, but Bunty still wouldn't go through the gates. "You're a bit shyer than your sister, aren't you?"

Bunty whinnied and twitched her ears. Bea gently tapped her heels against the pony's flanks and at last Bunty walked through the gate.

"Good girl, Bunty!" Bea whispered as they trotted along the palace drive.

Most of the guests were clustered around the picnic table. Natasha spotted Bea first and she rushed over, saying, "Why have you taken that pony from the stables, Bea? You know you weren't supposed to."

Bea climbed down from the pony's back and held the reins tightly. "This isn't the same pony. This is a different one."

"Honestly! Aren't you in enough

trouble already?" Natasha rolled her eyes. "You weren't allowed to keep the first animal, so you fetch another one straight away."

"It's not like that!" Bea stroked Bunty, who looked as if she was about to bolt. "Look, I'm really sorry about your dress—"

"What will dad say?" interrupted Natasha. "Chef Darou had to start making a whole new trifle after what your last pony did."

Before Bea could answer, the crowd parted and King George marched through. A lady, wearing a red T-shirt with *Stray Animal Services* on it, followed him, leading Sandy by the reins. The king saw Bea with Bunty and stopped in surprise. The ponies spotted each other at the same moment and neighed joyfully.

King George looked from one pony to the other. "Beatrice, what on earth…"

"Dad, I never meant to keep a stray pony here during the garden party. I'm really sorry about everything!" Bea felt tears prick her eyes and she wiped them away. "It was all a mistake… I thought I'd left Sandy at the farm but I'd got muddled because there are two ponies!" She explained what had happened when Sandy got scared by the snake and ran away.

By the time she'd finished explaining, Keira and Mr Morley had arrived. "So we got mixed up because the ponies look so alike," finished Bea.

"They're almost exactly the same." Keira looked from Sandy to Bunty. "The only difference is that Bunty's a little smaller and Sandy has larger grey spots on her back."

Mr Morley bowed his head to the king. "Good afternoon, Your Majesty. I'm very grateful to these girls for helping me find Bella. If it wasn't for them, she might still be wandering around on the beach."

"I see!" King George wrinkled his brow. "So, you're the ponies' owner then. And which one is Bella?"

"I've been calling her Sandy because she rolled about on the beach and got covered in sand," said Bea with a smile.

Sandy whickered and nibbled Bea's hair.

"I can see how much she likes you," Mr Morley told Bea. "You seem to have a knack with ponies."

The king's stern face softened a little. "I think Beatrice has a knack with all animals. THAT has been part of the problem!"

"I'll always be glad that she found little Bella," said Mr Morley. "These ponies were meant for my granddaughters to ride. They've been restless ever since the girls moved away. They just don't get ridden very much anymore."

An idea lit up Bea's mind like sunshine on a cloudy day. "What if Keira and I came to ride them? Then

 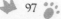

they wouldn't feel so restless. We could look after them too – brush their coats and manes. I've watched the grooms taking care of the royal horses so I think I know what to do."

King George sighed. "I'm afraid that's not possible, Beatrice. Farms are busy places and I'm sure you'd be in the way."

"I'd be happy for them to visit, Sire," said Mr Morley. "In fact, they'd be doing me a favour. These ponies need love and care, and I have a whole herd of cows to look after. I just don't have the time!"

Bea gazed at her dad and held her breath.

"Very well," the king said at last. "You may go to the farm to ride the ponies... on one condition. I shall buy you some riding boots and a riding hat that fits properly, and you *must* wear them."

"Thanks, Dad!" Bea hugged him before turning to Keira. "You'll ride with me, won't you?"

Keira beamed. "I'd love to!"

Sandy nibbled the king's arm and he brushed his sleeve hastily before turning to the lady from Stray Animal Services. "I'm sorry to have wasted your time. Would you like to stay and enjoy the party?"

The lady smiled. "Thank you, Your Majesty. I'm just glad the ponies will be back where they belong." She handed Sandy's broken reins to Mr Morley.

"Excuse me!" Mrs Stickler's voice cut through the crowd. "Make way, please." She appeared carrying a second trifle — even more splendid than the one before — with swirls of chocolate cream and fresh strawberries on top.

The trifle wobbled as the housekeeper set it carefully down on the picnic table. She scowled when she spotted Sandy and Bunty. "More ponies! Sire, is this good idea?"

Mr Morley, who hadn't noticed Mrs Stickler's grim face, rubbed his hands together happily. "That pudding looks delicious! You know – my ponies are very fond of a bowlful of trifle!"

"We know!" said Bea and Keira, giggling.

The laughter spread around the crowd and Sandy joined in with a loud whinny.

Chapter Nine
Pony Girls

Everyone had a wonderful time at the Royal Garden Party, except for Mrs Stickler who didn't even cheer up when Bea replaced all the nibbled flowers on the tables with fresh pink roses. The trifle was a great success, and Bea and Keira managed two bowlfuls each. Alfie ate four helpings before complaining that his stomach hurt.

Bea helped King George give out

the prizes. Mr Patel won an award for helping out his neighbours and Mrs Cherry was given another for growing delicious vegetables. Everyone agreed that it had been a lovely garden party – even better than the year before.

The next day, Keira arrived early at Ruby Palace. She and Bea went to the royal stables to have a lesson in pony care from the head groom, Sally. The groom had tied up Peppermint, one of the calmest horses in the stable, for them to practise on.

Bea's stomach gave a somersault as she waited for Sally to collect all the grooming equipment. She'd watched the stable hands lots of times, but she'd never had a proper lesson on looking after a pony before.

"It's important to groom a pony

carefully, especially after riding them,"
Sally told the girls. "First, use the dandy
brush to remove any mud like this." She
showed them how to use different brushes
to groom Peppermint, before using a
damp sponge to clean around the horse's
eyes and muzzle.

"Using a hoof pick is really
important." Sally explained how to get
loose stones out of a horse's hooves. Lastly,
she showed them how to brush and plait
a mane. By the time they'd finished,
Peppermint's mane looked beautiful and
her coat was gleaming.

"You've done a wonderful job," Sally
said, nodding approvingly. "I think
you're ready to groom Mr Morley's
ponies."

"Thanks for teaching us!" Bea grabbed
her riding hat, fizzing with excitement.

"Come on, Keira! Mr Morley said we could visit as early as we liked."

Bea and Keira rushed down the lane to Silver Gate Farm. Mr Morley was already out in the fields looking after the cows and he gave the girls a cheery wave. Sandy came trotting over straight away while Bunty ducked her head shyly.

"Hello Sandy!" Bea stroked the pony's neck and giggled when the little horse nibbled her hair. "I know you're meant to be called Bella but I think Sandy suits you better."

Keira gently rubbed Bunty's nose and offered her an apple that she'd brought from the café. Then she strapped on the riding hat that she'd borrowed from the royal stables. Bunty crunched the apple, her tail swishing.

The girls brushed the ponies the way Sally had showed them, before putting on the saddles and headcollars. Sandy's ears pricked as soon as Bea fastened her collar. She whinnied happily and stamped her feet.

"Stay still a minute, Sandy," Bea said, laughing. "I've got to make sure everything's done properly."

With her saddle strapped on, Sandy pranced over to the gate and stood there, waiting for Bea.

Keira tightened her pony's headcollar. "There you are, Bunty. You're ready too."

Bea and Keira rode the ponies down the lane. Sandy stepped forward eagerly, but Bunty tossed her head and shied away when a cyclist rode past.

Keira climbed down and took hold of the reins. "Let's lead them down the hill. I don't think Bunty likes the noise and traffic."

"Good idea," said Bea, climbing down from Sandy's back.

Bunty's ears pricked up as soon as they reached the seafront. The golden sand gleamed in the bright sunshine and the palm trees swayed in the breeze. Bea scrambled on to Sandy's back and the pony sprang forward, whinnying.

"Wait for me!" Keira climbed on to

Bunty's back and urged the little horse forward.

Sandy reached the sea first and galloped into the shallows. Her hooves sent glittering spray flying into the air. Bunty followed and the two ponies raced across the beach together.

Bea pulled on Sandy's reins as they reached the other side. "Whoa, Sandy!"

Sandy whickered and started pulling clumps of grass from the cliff.

"Just think!" Bea leaned forward to stroke the pony's neck. "We can spend the whole summer looking after the ponies. We can ride on the beach or at the farm every day!"

"Don't forget playing with Rosie and taking care of your kitten!" said Keira, grinning. "You have lots of animals to look after now. Do you think you'll have time for any new ones?"

"Don't worry! I'll always have time for more animals," Bea said firmly.

The girls turned the ponies around and cantered back along the beach. Bea's heart skipped as Sandy sped up and her hooves thundered on the warm golden sand.